For Richard, Willow, Camella, Alexander
and Uncle Scronce

N.M.

For Marcella, Tania, Troy and Marlin

G.F.

Magabala Books

BIP THE SNAPPING BUNGAROO

Narelle McRobbie

illustrated by Grace Fielding

Once upon a time there lived a happy little Bungaroo named Bip. Nowadays we know the Bungaroo as a turtle. Bip lived in a beautiful billabong beneath the shade of the gumtrees and by a rippling stream. Each morning the wallabies, echidnas, kangaroos, emus and many other animals would go to the water's edge to drink the fresh water and to feast on the luscious green grass.

About that time too Bip peeped out of his shell to greet the new morning. First he stretched his arms high into the air, toddled down to the stream and took one gigantic leap into the water. Then he swam once across and once back to wake himself up and feel fresh for the coming day. Then he made his way back to his favourite rock to dry in the morning sun and to *SNAP* his little jaws until he fell fast asleep. Ever since Bip could remember he could *SNAP SNAP*. Bip was very proud of his *SNAP SNAP SNAP* !

Each morning all of the other animals would listen for the familiar sound of Bip's *SNAP* and there was never a day gone by when the other animals would not say to each other, "Isn't the Bungaroo quite *SNAPPY?*" or "Isn't he a *SNAP* ahead of the rest?" All this talk made Bip feel proud to be a Bungaroo.

One morning Bip got up early, took his swim and went to dry and *SNAP*. The little Bungaroo *SNAPPED* here and he *SNAPPED* there, and he *SNAP SNAP SNAPPED* into the thin air.

Bip was having great fun, but all this activity made him feel tired, so he tucked his head into his shell and went travelling into his dreams.

Bip was far into dreamtime when Mother Kangaroo came bounding up to ask him an important favour. "Oh my," she exclaimed, "Bip is far into his dreams and it would be rude to wake him, as he looks so peaceful resting."

She stood there for a minute scratching her chin and thinking of what she should do. "Ah," she said, "I know just the thing." And away she went to collect some pebbles from the stream to make a pebbled gum leaf note, so when Bip awoke he would know what Mother Kangaroo's visit was all about.

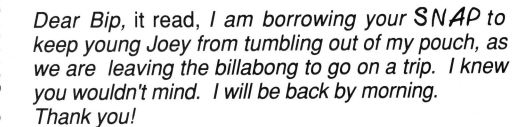

Dear Bip, it read, *I am borrowing your* SN𝒜P *to keep young Joey from tumbling out of my pouch, as we are leaving the billabong to go on a trip. I knew you wouldn't mind. I will be back by morning. Thank you!*

signed Mother Kangaroo

"There," she said, "Bip won't be too worried when he wakes up." She stooped down and, reaching into his shell, very carefully took the SNAP out.

Then Mother Kangaroo SNAPPED the SNAP onto her pouch, locking it securely, which gave young Joey only enough room to peep his little head out.

"This is just right," she thought as she hopped over Bip, but as she did so her long, strong tail hit the pebbled gum leaf note! Her tail sent the gum leaves and pebbles scattering. Mother Kangaroo did not know what she had done, as she was too busy adjusting her pouch and thinking of the long trip beyond the billabong.

It was way past lunch time when Bip awoke.

He was feeling mighty hungry. He opened his eyes wide and looked around. "What's this?" he said to himself, looking at the scattered pebbles and gum leaves. "Where did all these come from?" Bip asked in a puzzled voice.

He rubbed his eyes to be sure that he was not seeing things. The note that Mother Kangaroo had left was in bits and pieces, more of a jigsaw puzzle than a note. All Bip could do was look and scratch his head in amazement.

This was all the note read:
tum..ling out of my pouch........... leavin.. the billabong .... mind. .... you ....
signed Mo..er K....roo.

"I am too hungry to think about this now," Bip thought to himself as food kept flashing into his mind. So off he went to have something to eat.

The sun was almost setting when Bip returned from his long meal. His tummy was full and he was feeling content. He climbed onto his rock to ponder upon the mysterious pebbled gum leaf note that lay scattered on the rock. "It must be here for a reason," he thought. "But what can the reason be?" He moved his head this way and that way, trying to figure the message out. But it wasn't easy!

"This can wait until tomorrow," he said sleepily. Lazily he tucked his head into his shell and went once again into dreamtime.

The very next morning Bip awoke early, took his swim and then climbed back onto his rock to $SNAP$ and dry. He opened his jaws wide, but nothing came out. He tried again and still nothing happened. He stretched his neck, cleared his throat, and tried again!

Not a single snap could be heard.

Bip sat on his rock, turning his thoughts over in his mind. Now all of the other animals that listened for Bip's $SNAP$ $SNAP$ waited and waited. They came to see if the little Bungaroo had awoken.

Bip was in deep thought and did not hear the other animals coming up to check what was wrong, as by this time any other morning Bip would be in full swing $SNAP$ $SNAP$ $SNAPPING$. It was very unusual for Bip to be so quiet.

"Good morning," said a soft little voice. Bip looked up, "Oh hello Buba." There stood the tall emu. "Why are you not *SNAP SNAP SNAPPING* today?" Buba inquired. "I don't know," was Bip's reply.

Just then the twin wallaby sisters, Jilla and Roo, butted in, "Is there something wrong with your throat?" Again Bip's answer was the same.

"Can we help out in any way?" asked Coco Koala who had been sitting on a nearby gumtree having her breakfast. "I don't think so. I'll just have to work this problem out for myself," said Bip, but all the concerned animals kept on asking questions and answering themselves. No one could solve the mystery of the missing *SNAP*.

Bip just sat on his rock speechless and listened to their voices get louder and louder and louder.

Up bounded Mother Kangaroo and Joey. "What's all the commotion?" she asked Coco Koala, who was perched high in the gumtree. "This morning," Coco said as she swallowed a mouthful of gum leaves, "Bip went for his swim and then to his rock to dry and SNAP SNAP and wallah, not even a snap! Now all of his bush friends are trying to help him figure out where it has gone."

"Oh!" said Mother Kangaroo, "I can fix that problem straight away." And with one gigantic leap she hopped over all of the other animals and came down with a thud next to Bip. Silence fell as all the animals looked around in surprise.

"Good morning Bip," said Mother Kangaroo. "I see you didn't get the note that I left here."
"No," was Bip's reply.

"I came by yesterday," she said, "to borrow your *SNAP* to keep young Joey from tumbling out of my pouch and I knew you wouldn't mind. But I must say I wonder what could have become of that pebbled gum leaf note?"

"Dear, dear little Bungaroo," said Mother Kangaroo with a sigh, "You must have been worried out of your wits and I am terribly sorry."

After she had finished the whole story Bip said, "It's okay because I am glad my *SNAP* was of some use and I am proud more than ever you came to me for help." Mother Kangaroo turned to Bip and blinked her big beautiful eyelashes and said, "Bip Bungaroo you are a true friend indeed and I am very, very glad that you're mine." With these words all of Bip's bush friends who were standing round gave a loud cheer like no other cheer you have ever heard before.

Then Mother Kangaroo reached down to her pouch. She un*SNAPPED* the *SNAP* and carefully handed it to Bip. When everyone had left and gone their separate ways, Bip opened his jaws wide and gave the loudest

SNAP

you ever did hear - so loud that it echoed throughout the billabong. For Bip was the happiest and proudest little Bungaroo -

SNAP **SNAP** **SNAP**

First published by Magabala Books Aboriginal Corporation,
Broome, Western Australia, 1990.

Magabala Books receives financial assistance from the Government of Western
Australia, through the Department for the Arts.
This publication is assisted by the Australia Council, the Australian Government's
arts funding and advisory body, and the Aboriginal and Torres Strait Islander
Commission.

Designer Carol Tang Wei
Editor Peter Bibby
Production Coordinator Merrilee Lands
Printed by Tien Wah Press, Singapore
Typeset in Helvetica

National Library of Australia
Cataloguing-in-publication data

McRobbie, Narelle, 1965-
        Bip, the Snapping Bungaroo.

        ISBN 0 9588101 5 X

        1. Aborigines, Australian - Legends.
        1. Fielding, Grace, 1948-   11. Title.

398.20899915

NARELLE McROBBIE, who is of Pacific Island and Aboriginal descent, was brought up on the Atherton Tableland in Far North Queensland, where she still lives with her husband and three children. Narelle's knowledge of her father's tribal group, Yidin, was taught to her by her parents' families and other Yidin people living in the area. Her love of writing short stories for children has been furthered by her commitment to keeping the language alive. 'Bungaroo' is their word for 'turtle'. This is her first book.

GRACE FIELDING was raised at the St Francis Xavier Mission School at Wandering, Western Australia, and later went to live in Perth. Her interest in art and sketching has developed since moving to Broome with her four children in 1987, and she is now emerging as one of the Kimberley's many exciting artists. Known for her unique painting style that combines traditional dot art with contemporary images, Grace is also gaining a reputation for her fabric screen-printing.